This igloo book belongs to:

....

Published in 2017
by Igloo Books Ltd
Cottage Farm
Sywell
NN6 0BJ
www.igloobooks.com

HUN001 0517
4 6 8 10 12 11 9 7 5
ISBN 978-1-78557-087-2

Illustrated by Belinda Strong, Lindsey Sagar, and Louise Wright

Printed and manufactured in China

My First Treasury of Nursery Rhymes

igloobooks

Contents

Old MacDonald

Old MacDonald had a farm, E-I-E-I-O.
And on that farm he had some ducks, E-I-E-I-O.
With a quack-quack here and a quack-quack there.
Here a quack, there a quack, everywhere a quack-quack.
Old MacDonald had a farm, E-I-E-I-O.

Old MacDonald had a farm, E-I-E-I-O.
And on that farm, he had some cows, E-I-E-I-O.
With a moo-moo here and a moo-moo there.
Here a moo, there a moo, everywhere a moo-moo.
Old MacDonald had a farm, E-I-E-I-O.

Old MacDonald had a farm, E-I-E-I-O.
And on that farm, he had some sheep, E-I-E-I-O.
With a baa-baa here and a baa-baa there.
Here a baa, there a baa, everywhere a baa-baa.
Old MacDonald had a farm, E-I-E-I-O.

Old MacDonald had a farm, E-I-E-I-O.
And on that farm, he had some pigs, E-I-E-I-O.
With an oink-oink here and an oink-oink there.
Here an oink, there an oink, everywhere an oink-oink.
Old MacDonald had a farm, E-I-E-I-O.

Baa, Baa, Black Sheep

Baa, baa, black sheep,
Have you any wool?
Yes, sir. Yes, sir,
Three bags full.
One for the master,
And one for the dame,
And one for the little boy,
Who lives down the lane.

The Gingerbread Man

Run, run, as fast as you can.
You can't catch me,
I'm the Gingerbread Man.

Hot Cross Buns

Hot cross buns, hot cross buns.
One a penny, two a penny, hot cross buns.
If you have no daughters, give them to your sons.
One a penny, two a penny, hot cross buns.

Gingerbread

Mix and stir and pat it in the pan.
I'm going to make a gingerbread man.
With a nose so neat,
And a smile so sweet,
And gingerbread shoes,
On his gingerbread feet.

The Muffin Man

Oh, do you know the Muffin Man,
The Muffin Man,
The Muffin Man?
Do you know the Muffin Man,
Who lives on Drury Lane?

Oh, yes, I know the Muffin Man,
The Muffin Man,
The Muffin Man.
Yes, I know the Muffin Man,
Who lives on Drury Lane.

11

Jack and Jill

Jack and Jill went up the hill,
To fetch a pail of water.
Jack fell down and broke his crown,
And Jill came tumbling after.

Mary, Mary, Quite Contrary

Mary, Mary, quite contrary,
How does your garden grow?
With silver bells and cockle shells,
And pretty maids all in a row.

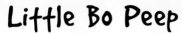

Little Bo Peep

Litte Bo Peep has lost her sheep,
And doesn't know where to find them.
Leave them alone and they'll come home,
Bringing their tails behind them.

Humpty Dumpty

Humpty Dumpty sat on a wall.
Humpty Dumpty had a great fall.
All the king's horses and all the king's men,
Couldn't put Humpty together again.

Hey, Diddle, Diddle

Hey, diddle, diddle,
The cat and the fiddle.
The cow jumped over the moon.
The little dog laughed to see such sport,
And the dish ran away with the spoon.

14

Old King Cole

Old King Cole was a merry old soul,
And a merry old soul was he.
He called for his pipe and he called for his bowl,
And he called for his fiddlers three.
Every fiddler, he had a fiddle,
And a very fine fiddle had he.
Oh, there's none so rare, as can compare,
With King Cole and his fiddlers three.

Doodle, Doodle, Doo

Doodle, doodle, doo,
The princess lost her shoe.
Her highness hopped,
The fiddler stopped,
Not knowing what to do.

15

See-saw, Margery Daw

See-saw, Margery Daw,
Jacky shall have a new master.
He shall have but a penny a day,
Because he can't work any faster.

Ring Around the Rosie

Ring around the rosie
A pocket full of posies.
Ashes, ashes,
We all fall down.

Dingly, Dangly Scarecrow

I'm a dingly, dangly scarecrow,
With a flippy, floppy hat.
I can shake my hands like this,
I can shake my feet like that.

Bow, wow, wow

Bow, wow, wow,
Whose dog art thou?
Little Tom Tinker's dog,
Bow, wow, wow.

One Potato, Two Potato

One potato, two potato,
Three potato, four.
Five potato, six potato,
Seven potato more.

Little Tommy Tucker

Little Tommy Tucker,
Sings for his supper.
What shall we give him?
White bread and butter.
How shall he cut it without any knife?
How will he marry without any wife?

Jack Sprat

Jack Sprat could eat no fat,
His wife could eat no lean,
And so between them both, you see,
They licked the platter clean.

Sippity Sup

Sippity sup, sippity sup,
Bread and milk from a china cup.
Bread and milk from a bright silver spoon,
Made of a piece of the bright silver moon.
Sippity sup, sippity sup,
Sippity, sippity sup.

If Wishes Were Horses

If wishes were horses,
Beggars would ride.
If turnips were watches,
I would wear one by my side.

A Swarm of Bees

A swarm of bees in May,
Is worth a load of hay.
A swarm of bees in June,
Is worth a silver spoon.
A swarm of bees in July,
Is not worth a fly.

Little Cock Sparrow

A little cock sparrow sat on a tree,
Looking as happy as happy could be.
Till a boy came by with a bow and arrow,
Says he, "I will shoot the little cock sparrow."

"His body will make me a nice, little stew,
And his giblets will make me a little pie, too."
Says the little cock sparrow, "I'll be shot if I stay."
So he clapped his wings and then flew away.

Butterfly, Butterfly

Butterfly, butterfly, flutter around.
Butterfly, butterfly, touch the ground.
Butterfly, butterfly, fly so free.
Butterfly, butterfly, land on me.
Butterfly, butterfly, reach the sky.
Butterfly, butterfly, say goodbye.

The Lion and the Unicorn

The lion and the unicorn were fighting for the crown.
The lion beat the unicorn all around the town.
Some gave them white bread and some gave them brown.
Some gave them plum cake and drummed them out of town.

The Animal Fair

I went to the animal fair,
The birds and the beasts were there.
The big baboon by the light of the moon,
Was combing his auburn hair.

You ought to have seen the monkey,
He jumped on the elephant's trunk.
The elephant sneezed and fell to his knees,
And what became of the monkey?

Eeny, Meeny, Miny, Moe

Eeny, meeny, miny, moe,
Catch a tiger by the toe.
If he hollers, let him go,
Eeny, meeny, miny, moe.

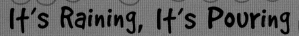

It's Raining, It's Pouring

It's raining, it's pouring,
The old man is snoring.
He went to bed,
And bumped his head,
And couldn't get up in the morning.

Doctor Foster

Doctor Foster went to Gloucester,
In a shower of rain.
He stepped in a puddle,
Right up to his middle,
And never went there again.

Rain, Rain, Go Away

Rain, rain, go away,
Come again another day.
Little Johnny wants to play.

Rain on the Green Grass

Rain on the green grass,
And rain on the tree.
Rain on the rooftop,
But not on me.

25

Three Blind Mice

Three blind mice, three blind mice.
See how they run, see how they run.
They all ran after the farmer's wife,
Who chased after them with a carving knife.
Did you ever see such a thing in your life,
As three blind mice?

Tommy Tittlemouse

Little Tommy Tittlemouse,
Lived in a little house.
He caught fishes,
In other men's ditches.

Itsy Bitsy Spider

Itsy Bitsy Spider,
Climbed up the waterspout.
Down came the rain,
And washed the spider out.
Out came the sunshine,
And dried up all the rain.
And Itsy Bitsy Spider,
Climbed up the spout again.

Purple Cow

I never saw a purple cow.
I never hope to see one.
But I can tell you, anyhow,
I'd rather see than be one.

The Boy in the Barn

A little boy went into the barn,
And lay down on some hay.
An owl came out and flew about,
And the little boy ran away.

28

Mary Had a Little Lamb

Mary had a little lamb,
Whose fleece was white as snow.
And everywhere that Mary went,
The lamb was sure to go.

He followed her to school one day,
That was against the rule.
It made the children laugh and play,
To see a lamb at school.

And so the teacher turned it out,
But still it lingered near.
And waited patiently about,
Till Mary did appear.

"Why does the lamb love Mary so?"
The eager children cry.
"Why, Mary loves the lamb, you know,"
The teacher did reply.

Little Robin Redbreast

Little Robin Redbreast sat upon a tree,
Up went the pussycat and down went he.
Down came pussy and away Robin ran,
Says Little Robin Redbreast, "Catch me if you can."

Birds of a feather

Birds of a feather flock together,
And so do pigs and swine.
Rats and mice will have their choice,
And so will I have mine.

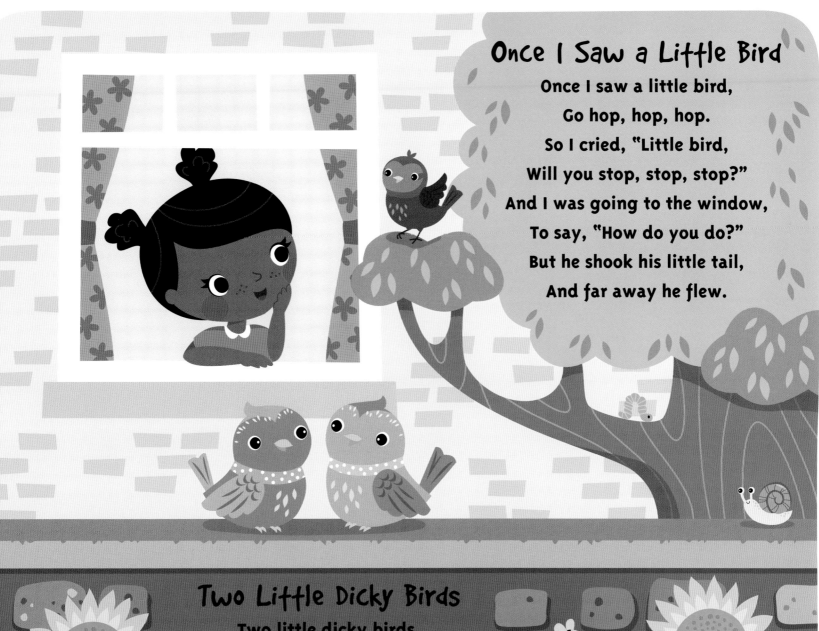

Once I Saw a Little Bird

Once I saw a little bird,
Go hop, hop, hop.
So I cried, "Little bird,
Will you stop, stop, stop?"
And I was going to the window,
To say, "How do you do?"
But he shook his little tail,
And far away he flew.

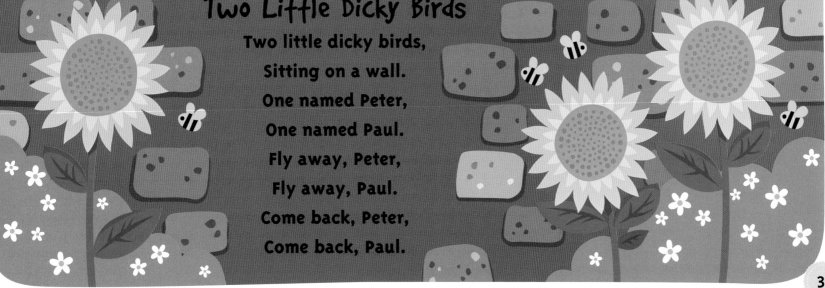

Two Little Dicky Birds

Two little dicky birds,
Sitting on a wall.
One named Peter,
One named Paul.
Fly away, Peter,
Fly away, Paul.
Come back, Peter,
Come back, Paul.

Tommy Snooks

As Tommy Snooks and Bessie Brooks,
Were walking out one Sunday.
Says Tommy Snooks to Bessie Brooks,
"Tomorrow will be Monday."

Daffy Down Dilly

Daffy Down Dilly,
Has come to town,
In a yellow petticoat,
And a green gown.

Higglety, Pigglety, Pop

Higglety, pigglety, pop.
The dog has eaten the mop.
The pig's in a hurry,
The cat's in a flurry,
Higglety, pigglety, pop.

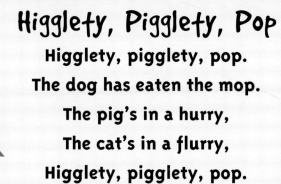

To Market, To Market

To market, to market, to buy a fat pig,
Home again, home again, jiggety-jig.

To market, to market, to buy a fat hog,
Home again, home again, jiggety-jog.

To market, to market, to buy a plum bun,
Home again, home again, market is done.

The King of France

The King of France went up the hill,
With twenty thousand men.
The King of France came down the hill,
And never went up again.

The Queen of Hearts

The Queen of Hearts,
She made some tarts,
All on a summer's day.

The Knave of Hearts,
He stole the tarts,
And took them clean away.

The King of Hearts
Called for the tarts,
And beat the Knave full sore.

The Knave of Hearts,
Brought back the tarts,
And vowed he'd steal no more.

King of the Castle

I'm the king of the castle,
Get down, you dirty rascal.
Get down, get down,
I'm the king of the castle.

Little Girl and Queen

Little girl, little girl, where have you been?
Gathering roses to give to the Queen.
Little girl, little girl, what gave she you?
She gave me a diamond as big as my shoe.

Lucy Locket

Lucy Locket lost her pocket,
Kitty Fisher found it.
Not a penny was there in it,
Only ribbon round it.

Girls and Boys, Come Out to Play

Girls and boys, come out to play.
The moon will shine as bright as day.
Leave your supper and leave your sleep,
And come with your play friends into the street.
Come with a whoop, come with a call.
Come with a good will or not at all.
Up the ladder and down the wall,
A halfpenny roll will serve us all.
You'll find milk and I'll find flour,
And we'll have a pudding in half an hour.

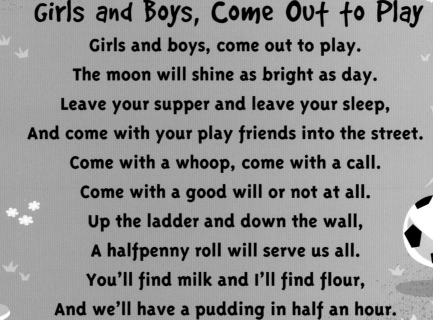

Georgie Porgie

Georgie Porgie, pudding and pie,
Kissed the girls and made them cry.
When the boys came out to play,
Georgie Porgie ran away.

Girls Are Dandy

Girls are dandy, made of candy,
That's what little girls are made of.
Boys are rotten, made of cotton,
That's what little boys are made of.

Pease Porridge Hot

Pease porridge hot, pease porridge cold.
Pease porridge in the pot, nine days old.
Some like it hot, some like it cold.
Some like it in the pot, nine days old.

Pat-a-cake

Pat-a-cake, pat-a-cake, baker's man.
Bake me a cake as fast as you can.
Roll it, pat it, and mark it with a 'b',
Put it in the oven for baby and me.

38

Little Polly Flinders

Little Polly Flinders
Sat among the cinders,
Warming her pretty, little toes.
Her mother came and caught her,
Told off her little daughter,
For spoiling her nice, new clothes.

Little Betty Blue

Little Betty Blue,
Lost her holiday shoe.
What can little Betty do?
Give her another,
To match the other,
And then she may walk in two.

39

Rock-a-bye Baby

Rock-a-bye baby on the treetop.
When the wind blows, the cradle will rock.
When the bough breaks, the cradle will fall.
And down will come baby, cradle and all.

Little Miss Muffet

Little Miss Muffet,
Sat on a tuffet,
Eating her curds and whey.
Along came a spider,
Who sat down beside her,
And frightened Miss Muffet away.

The Apple Tree

Here is the tree with leaves so green,
Here are the apples that hang between.
When the wind blows, the apples fall.
Here is a basket to gather them all.

I Had a Little Nut Tree

I had a little nut tree,
Nothing would it bear.
But a silver nutmeg,
And a golden pear.
The King of Spain's daughter,
Came to visit me.
And all for the sake,
Of my little nut tree.

Her dress was made of crimson,
Jet black was her hair.
She asked me for my nut tree,
And my golden pear.
I said, "So fair a princess,
Never did I see.
I'll give you all the fruit,
From my little nut tree."

41

Elsie Marley

Elsie Marley is grown so fine.
She won't get up to feed the swine.
But lies in bed till eight or nine.
Lazy Elsie Marley.

Barber, Barber

Barber, barber, shave a pig.
How many hairs to make a wig?
Four and twenty, that's enough.
Give the barber a pinch of snuff.

42

Monday's Child

Monday's child is fair of face,
Tuesday's child is full of grace.
Wednesday's child is full of woe,
Thursday's child has far to go.
Friday's child is loving and giving,
Saturday's child must work hard for a living.
But the child who is born on the Sabbath Day,
Is bonny and blithe and good and gay.

Five Little Ducks

Five little ducks,
Went out one day,
Over the hills and far away.
Mother duck said,
"Quack, quack, quack, quack."
But only four little ducks came back.

Four little ducks,
Went out one day,
Over the hills and far away.
Mother duck said,
"Quack, quack, quack, quack."
But only three little ducks came back.

Three little ducks,
Went out one day,
Over the hills and far away.
Mother duck said,
"Quack, quack, quack, quack."
But only two little ducks came back.

Two little ducks,
Went out one day,
Over the hills and far away.
Mother duck said,
"Quack, quack, quack, quack."
But only one little duck came back.

One little duck,
Went out one day,
Over the hills and far away.
Mother duck said,
"Quack, quack, quack, quack."
And all of the five little ducks came back.

A Duck and a Drake

A duck and a drake,
And a nice barley cake,
With a penny to pay the old baker.
A hop and a scotch,
Is another notch,
Slitherum, slitherum, take her.

This Little Piggy

This little piggy went to market,
This little piggy stayed at home.
This little piggy had roast beef,
This little piggy had none.
And this little piggy went,
"Wee, wee, wee," all the way home.

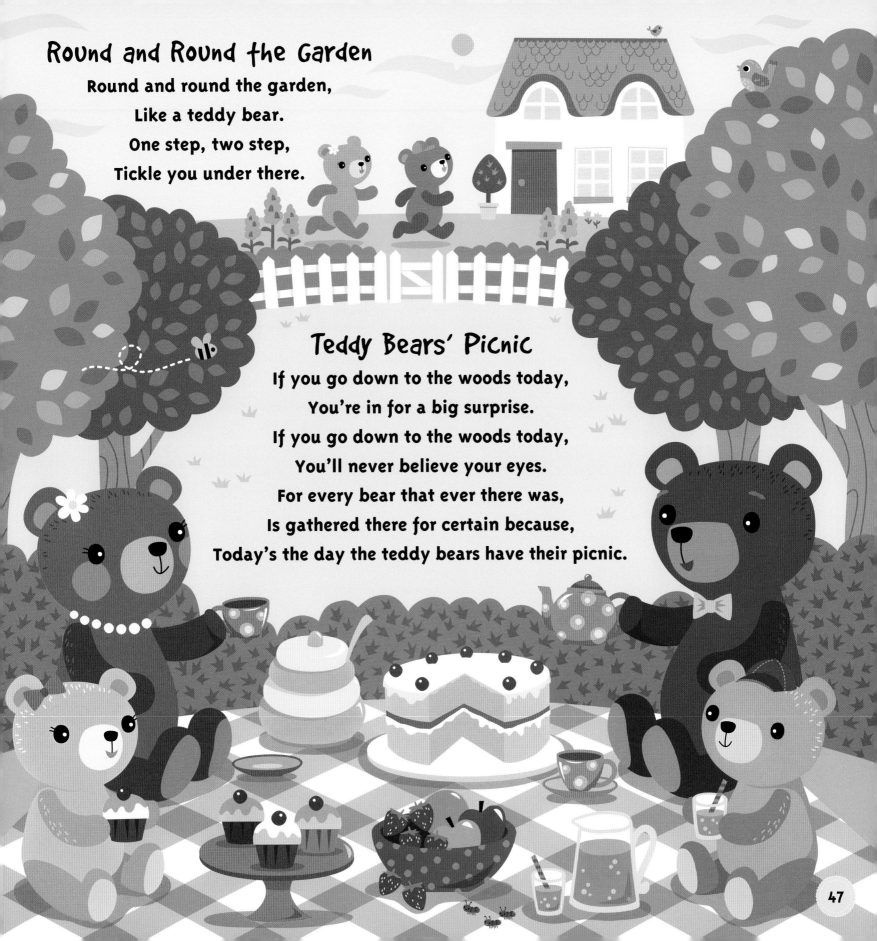

Round and Round the Garden

Round and round the garden,
Like a teddy bear.
One step, two step,
Tickle you under there.

Teddy Bears' Picnic

If you go down to the woods today,
You're in for a big surprise.
If you go down to the woods today,
You'll never believe your eyes.
For every bear that ever there was,
Is gathered there for certain because,
Today's the day the teddy bears have their picnic.

Kookaburra

Kookaburra sits on the old gum tree.
Merry, merry king of the bush is he.
Laugh, Kookaburra. Laugh, Kookaburra.
Gay your life must be.

Draw a Pail of Water

Draw a pail of water,
For my lady's daughter.
Her father's a king and her mother's a queen,
Her two little sisters are dressed in green.
Stamping grass and parsley,
Marigold leaves and daisies.
One rush, two rush.
Pray thee, fine lady,
Come under my bush.

The Grand Old Duke of York

Oh, the grand old Duke of York,
He had ten thousand men.
He marched them up to the top of the hill,
And he marched them down again.
And when they were up, they were up.
And when they were down, they were down.
And when they were only halfway up,
They were neither up nor down.

Sing a Song of Sixpence

Sing a song of sixpence,
A pocket full of rye.
Four and twenty blackbirds,
Baked in a pie.
When the pie was opened,
The birds began to sing,
"Wasn't that a dainty dish,
To set before the king?"

Here We Go Gathering

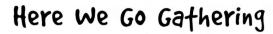

Here we go gathering nuts in May,
Nuts in May, nuts in May.
Here we go gathering nuts in May,
On a cold and frosty morning.

Who will you have for nuts in May,
Nuts in May, nuts in May?
Who will you have for nuts in May,
On a cold and frosty morning?

Who will you send to fetch her away,
Fetch her away, fetch her away?
Who will you send to fetch her away,
On a cold and frosty morning?

Tom and Jack will fetch her away,
Fetch her away, fetch her away.
Tom and Jack will fetch her away,
On a cold and frosty morning.

Fee-fi-fo-fum

Fee-fi-fo-fum,
I smell the blood of an Englishman.
Be he alive or be he dead,
I'll grind his bones to make my bread.

Up in the Green Orchard

Up in the green orchard, there is a green tree.
The finest of pippins that you may see.
The apples are ripe and ready to fall,
And Richard and Robin shall gather them all.

51

The Big Ship Sails

The big ship sails,
On the ally-ally-oh.
The ally-ally-oh.
Oh, the big ship sails,
On the ally-ally-oh.
On the last day of September.

Dance to Your Daddy

Dance to your daddy,
My bonny laddy,
Dance to your daddy,
My bonny lamb.

You shall have a fishy,
In a little dishy.
You shall have a fishy,
When the boat comes in.

You shall get a coaty,
And a pair of breeches,
And you'll get an eggy,
And a bit of ham.

52

A Sailor Went to Sea

A sailor went to sea, sea, sea,
To see what he could see, see, see,
And all that he could see, see, see,
Was the bottom of the deep, blue sea, sea, sea.

Bobby Shafto

Bobby Shafto went to sea,
Silver buckles on his knee.
He'll come back and marry me.
Bonny Bobby Shafto.

Bobby Shafto's bright and fair,
Combing out his auburn hair.
He's my friend forever more.
Bonny Bobby Shafto.

53

The Moon

The moon is round,
As round can be.
Two eyes, a nose,
And a mouth, like me.

Wee Willie Winkie

Wee Willie Winkie runs through the town,
Upstairs and downstairs in his nightgown.
Tapping at the window, crying through the lock,
"Are all the children in their beds,
Now it's eight o'clock?"

Little Boys

What are little boys made of?
What are little boys made of?
Slugs and snails,
And puppy dog tails.
That's what little boys are made of.

Little Girls

What are little girls made of?
What are little girls made of?
Sugar and spice,
And all things nice.
That's what little girls are made of.

Horsey, Horsey

Horsey, horsey, don't you stop.
Just let your feet go clippety-clop.
Your tail goes swish and the wheels go round.
Giddy up, we're homeward bound.

We're not in a hustle, we're not in a bustle.
Don't go tearing up the road.
We're not in a hurry, we're not in a flurry,
And we don't have a very heavy load.

Horsey, horsey, don't you stop.
Just let your feet go clippety-clop.
Your tail goes swish and the wheels go round.
Giddy up, we're homeward bound.

For Want of a Nail

For want of a nail, the shoe was lost.
For want of a shoe, the horse was lost.
For want of a horse, the rider was lost.
For want of a rider, the battle was lost.
For want of a battle, the kingdom was lost.
And all for the want of a horseshoe nail.

Yankee Doodle

Yankee Doodle went to town,
Riding on a pony.
Stuck a feather in his cap,
And called it macaroni.

Yankee Doodle, keep it up.
Yankee Doodle dandy.
Mind the music and the step,
And with the girls be handy.

Cobbler, Cobbler

Cobbler, cobbler, mend my shoe.
Get it done by half past two.
Half past two is much too late,
Get it done by half past eight.

The Cats Went Out

The cats went out to serenade,
And on a banjo they sweetly played.
And summer nights, they climbed a tree,
And sang, "My love, oh, come to me."

Pussycat, Pussycat

Pussycat, pussycat, where have you been?
I've been to London to visit the Queen.
Pussycat, pussycat, what did you do there?
I frightened a little mouse under her chair.

London Bridge

London Bridge is falling down,
Falling down, falling down.
London Bridge is falling down,
My fair lady.

Three Little Kittens

Three little kittens, they lost their mittens.
And they began to cry.
"Oh, Mother, dear, we sadly fear,
That we have lost our mittens."
"Lost your mittens? You naughty kittens.
Then you shall have no pie."
"Meow, meow, meow."
"Then you shall have no pie."

59

The Wheels on the Bus

The wheels on the bus go round and round,
Round and round, round and round.
The wheels on the bus go round and round,
All through the town.

The horn on the bus goes beep, beep, beep,
Beep, beep, beep, beep, beep, beep.
The horn on the bus goes beep, beep, beep,
All through the town.

The wipers on the bus go swish, swish, swish,
Swish, swish, swish, swish, swish, swish.
The wipers on the bus go swish, swish, swish,
All through the town.

The people on the bus go up and down,
Up and down, up and down.
The people on the bus go up and down,
All through the town.

Hickory, Dickory, Dock

Hickory, dickory, dock.
The mouse ran up the clock.
The clock struck one,
The mouse ran down.
Hickory, dickory, dock.

62

Old Mother Hubbard

Old Mother Hubbard,
Went to the cupboard,
To give her poor dog a bone.
But when she got there,
The cupboard was bare,
And so the poor dog had none.

Six Little Mice

Six little mice sat down to spin.
Kitty passed by and she peeped in.
"What are you doing, my little men?"
"Weaving coats for gentlemen."
"Shall I come in and cut off your threads?"
"No, no, Miss Kitty, you'd bite off our heads."
"Oh, no, I'll not. I'll help you to spin."
"That may be so, but you can't come in."

63

Five Fat Sausages

Five fat sausages sizzling in a pan,
One went pop and the others went bang.

Four fat sausages sizzling in a pan,
One went pop and the others went bang.

Three fat sausages sizzling in a pan,
One went pop and the others went bang.

Two fat sausages sizzling in a pan,
One went pop and the other went bang.

One fat sausage sizzling in a pan,
One went pop and none went bang.

No fat sausages sizzling in a pan.

There Was an Old Woman Who Lived in a Shoe

There was an old woman who lived in a shoe.

She had so many children, she didn't know what to do.

She gave them some soup and slices of bread.

She hugged them and kissed them,

Then put them to bed.

Rub-a-dub-dub

Rub-a-dub-dub,
Three men in a tub,
And who do you think they be?
The butcher, the baker,
The candlestick maker.
They all sailed out to sea.

If All the Seas Were One Sea

If all the seas were one sea, what a great sea that would be.
And if all the trees were one tree, what a great tree that would be.
And if all the axes were one axe, what a great axe that would be.
And if all the men were one man, what a great man that would be.
And if the great man took the great axe and cut down the great tree
And let it fall into the great sea, what a splish-splash that would be.

Tinker, Tailor

Tinker, tailor, soldier, sailor,
Rich man, poor man,
Beggar man, thief.

She Sells Seashells

She sells seashells on the seashore.
The shells she sells are seashells, I'm sure.
And if she sells seashells on the seashore,
Then I'm sure she sells seashore shells.

67

I Saw Three Ships

I saw three ships come sailing by,
Come sailing by, come sailing by.
I saw three ships come sailing by,
On New Year's Day in the morning.

And what do you think was in them then,
Was in them then, was in them then?
And what do you think was in them then,
On New Year's Day in the morning?

Three pretty girls were in them then,
Were in them then, were in them then.
Three pretty girls were in them then,
On New Year's Day in the morning.

One could whistle and one could sing,
And one could play the violin.
Such joy there was at my wedding,
On New Year's Day in the morning.

Come to the Window

Come to the window,
My baby, with me,
And look at the stars,
That shine on the sea.

There are two little stars,
That play bo-peep.
With two little fish,
Far down in the deep.

And two little frogs,
Cry, "Neap, neap, neap."
I see a dear baby,
That should be asleep.

Someone Came Knocking

Someone came knocking at my wee, small door,
Someone came knocking, I'm sure, sure, sure.
I listened, I opened, I looked to left and right,
But nought there was stirring in the still, dark night.

Only the busy beetle tap-tapping in the wall.
Only from the forest the screech-owl's call.
Only the cricket whistling while the dewdrops fall,
So I know not who came knocking, at all, at all, at all.

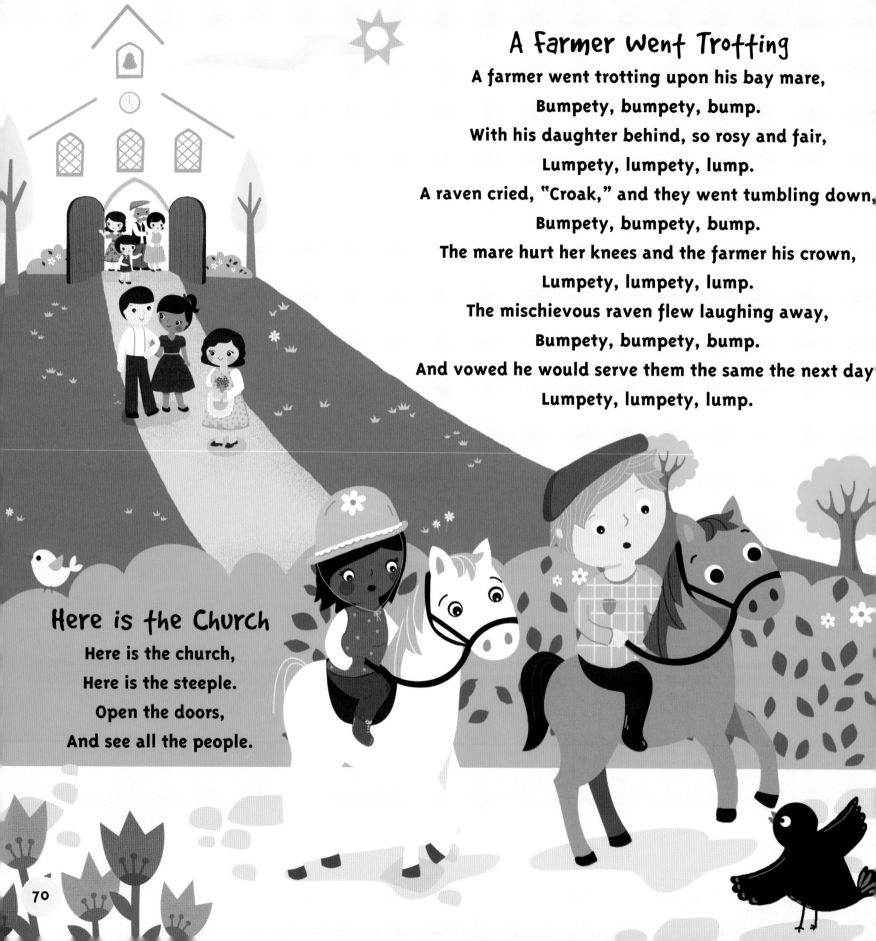

A farmer Went Trotting

A farmer went trotting upon his bay mare,
Bumpety, bumpety, bump.
With his daughter behind, so rosy and fair,
Lumpety, lumpety, lump.
A raven cried, "Croak," and they went tumbling down,
Bumpety, bumpety, bump.
The mare hurt her knees and the farmer his crown,
Lumpety, lumpety, lump.
The mischievous raven flew laughing away,
Bumpety, bumpety, bump.
And vowed he would serve them the same the next day
Lumpety, lumpety, lump.

Here is the Church

Here is the church,
Here is the steeple.
Open the doors,
And see all the people.

Row, Row, Row Your Boat

Row, row, row your boat,

Gently down the stream.

Merrily, merrily,

Merrily, merrily.

Life is but a dream.

Row, row, row your boat,

Gently down the stream.

If you see a crocodile,

Don't forget to scream.

Cross Patch

Cross Patch,
Draw the latch,
Sit by the fire and spin.
Take a cup and drink it up,
Then call your neighbors in.

Pop Goes the Weasel

All around the carpenter's bench,
The monkey chased the weasel.
That's the way the monkey goes.
Pop goes the weasel.

Polly, Put the Kettle On

Polly, put the kettle on,
Polly, put the kettle on,
Polly, put the kettle on.
We'll all have tea.

Sukey, take it off again,
Sukey, take it off again,
Sukey, take it off again.
They've all gone away.

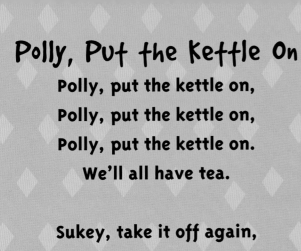

I'm a Little Teapot

I'm a little teapot, short and stout.
Here is my handle, here is my spout.
When I get all steamed up, hear me shout,
"Tip me up and pour me out."

Falling Leaves

All the leaves are falling down,
Orange, yellow, red, and brown.
Falling softly as they do,
Over me and over you.
All the leaves are falling down,
Orange, yellow, red, and brown.

Blow, Wind, Blow

Blow, wind, blow and go, mill, go.
That the miller may grind his corn.
That the baker may take it,
And into bread make it,
And bring us a loaf in the morn.

74

The North Wind Doth Blow

The North Wind doth blow,
And we shall have snow,
And what will poor robin do then,
Poor thing?
He'll sit in a barn,
And keep himself warm,
And hide his head under his wing,
Poor thing.

Red Sky at Night

Red sky at night,
Shepherd's delight.
Red sky in the morning,
Shepherd's warning.

The Ants Go Marching

The ants go marching one by one,
Hurrah, hurrah.
The ants go marching one by one,
Hurrah, hurrah.
The ants go marching one by one,
The little one stops to suck his thumb,
And they all go marching down,
To the ground,
To get out of the rain.
Boom, boom, boom, boom.

The ants go marching two by two,
Hurrah, hurrah.
The ants go marching two by two,
Hurrah, hurrah.
The ants go marching two by two,
The little one stops to tie her shoe,
And they all go marching down,
To the ground,
To get out of the rain.
Boom, boom, boom, boom.

The Bear Went Over the Mountain

The bear went over the mountain,
The bear went over the mountain,
The bear went over the mountain,
To see what he could see.

And all that he could see,
And all that he could see,
Was the other side of the mountain,
The other side of the mountain,
The other side of the mountain,
Was all that he could see.

Fuzzy Wuzzy

Fuzzy Wuzzy was a bear.
Fuzzy Wuzzy had no hair.
So, Fuzzy Wuzzy wasn't really fuzzy,
Was he?

The Owl and the Pussycat

The owl and the pussycat went to sea,
In a beautiful pea-green boat.
They took some honey and plenty of money,
Wrapped up in a five pound note.

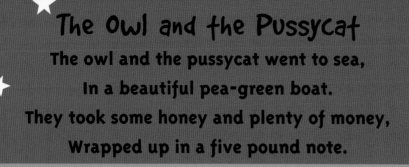

The owl looked up to the stars above,
And sang to a small guitar.
"Oh, lovely pussy. Oh, pussy, my love.
What a beautiful pussy you are, you are.
What a beautiful pussy you are."

Pussy said to the owl, "You elegant fowl,
How charmingly sweet you sing.
Oh, let us be married, too long we have tarried,
But what shall we do for a ring?"

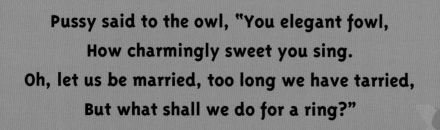

They sailed away for a year and a day,
To the land where the bong tree grows.
And there in a wood, a piggy-wig stood,
With a ring at the end of his nose, his nose,
With a ring at the end of his nose.

"Dear pig, are you willing to sell for one shilling,
Your ring?" Said the piggy, "I will."
So they took it away and were married next day,
By the turkey who lives on the hill.

They dined on mince and slices of quince,
Which they ate with a runcible spoon.
And hand in hand, on the edge of the sand,
They danced by the light of the moon, the moon,
They danced by the light of the moon.

Baby Dolly

Hush, baby, my dolly, I pray you don't cry,
And I'll give you some bread and some milk, by and by.
Or perhaps you like custard, or maybe a tart,
Then to either you're welcome with all my heart.

Babies

Come to the land where the babies grow,
Like flowers in the green, green grass.
Tiny babes that swing and crow,
Whenever the warm winds pass,
And laugh at their own bright eyes aglow,
In a fairy looking glass.

Come to the sea where the babies sail,
In ships of shining pearl.
Borne to the west by a golden gale,
Of sunbeams all awhirl,
And perhaps a baby brother will sail,
To you, my little girl.

Bye, Baby Bunting

Bye, baby Bunting,
Daddy's gone a-hunting,
To get a little rabbit skin,
To wrap my baby Bunting in.

Sleep, Baby, Sleep

Sleep, baby, sleep.
Your father tends the sheep,
Your mother shakes the dreamland tree,
And from it fall sweet dreams for thee.
Sleep, baby, sleep.
Sleep, baby, sleep.

81

One Man Went to Mow

One man went to mow, went to mow a meadow,
One man and his dog,
Went to mow a meadow.

Two men went to mow, went to mow a meadow,
Two men, one man, and his dog,
Went to mow a meadow.

Three men went to mow, went to mow a meadow,
Three men, two men, one man, and his dog,
Went to mow a meadow.

Four men went to mow, went to mow a meadow,
Four men, three men, two men, one man, and his dog,
Went to mow a meadow.

I Had a Little Pony

I had a little pony. His name was Dapple Gray.
I lent him to a lady to ride a mile away.
She whipped him, she thrashed him,
She rode him through the mire.
Now I would not lend my poor pony to any lady hire.

The Cock Crows

The cock crows in the morn,
To tell us to rise,
And he that lies late,
Will never be wise.

For early to bed,
And early to rise,
Is the way to be healthy,
And wealthy and wise.

Little Boy Blue

Little Boy Blue, come, blow your horn.
The sheep's in the meadow, the cow's in the corn.
Where's the little boy that looks after the sheep?
Under the haystack, fast asleep.

83

Grandmother Grundy

Oh, Grandmother Grundy,
Now what would you say,
If the katydids carried,
Your glasses away?

Carried them off,
To the top of the sky,
And used them to watch,
The eclipses go by?

A Needle and Thread

Old Mother Twitchett had but one eye,
And a long tail, which she let fly.
And every time she went through a gap,
A bit of her tail she left in a trap.

Dame Trot and Her Cat

Dame Trot and her cat,
Led a peaceable life,
When they were not troubled,
With other folks' strife.
When Dame had her dinner,
Pussy would wait,
And was sure to receive,
A nice piece from her plate.

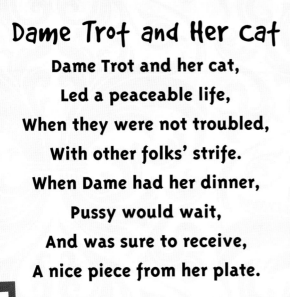

Grandma's Spectacles

These are Grandma's spectacles,
This is Grandma's hat.
This is the way she folds her hands,
And lays them on her lap.

Goosey, Goosey, Gander

Goosey, goosey, gander,
Where shall I wander?
Upstairs and downstairs,
And in my lady's chamber.
There I met an old man,
Who would not say his prayers.
I took him by the left leg,
And threw him down the stairs.

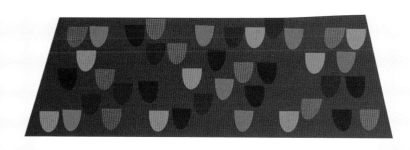

Three Gray Geese

Three gray geese,
In the green grass grazing.
Gray were the geese,
And green was the grass.

Oranges and Lemons

"Oranges and lemons," say the bells of St. Clement's.

"You owe me five farthings," say the bells of St. Martin's.

"When will you pay me?" say the bells of Old Bailey.

"When I grow rich," say the bells of Shoreditch.

"When will that be?" say the bells of Stepney.

"I do not know," says the great bell at Bow.

"Here comes a candle to light you to bed.

Here comes a chopper to chop off his head."

Little Jack Horner

Little Jack Horner sat in the corner,
Eating a Christmas pie.
He put in his thumb,
And pulled out a plum,
And said, "What a good boy am I."

Eat, Eat, Eat

Here come the sweet potatoes,
And here's the Sunday meat.
I guess we must be ready now,
To eat, eat, eat.

A Plum Pudding

Flour of England, fruit of Spain,
Met together in a shower of rain.
Put in a bag tied round with a string,
If you'll tell me this riddle,
I'll give you a ring.

Fairy Bread

Come up here, oh, dusty feet.
Here is fairy bread to eat.
Here in my retiring room,
Children, you may dine,
On the golden smell of broom,
And the shade of pine.
And when you have eaten well,
Fairy stories hear and tell.

Jack be Nimble

Jack be nimble,
Jack be quick.
Jack jump over,
The candlestick.

I See the Moon

I see the moon,
And the moon sees me.
God bless the moon,
And God bless me.

The Man in the Moon

The man in the moon came tumbling down,
And asked the way to Norwich.
He went by the south and burned his mouth,
With eating cold pease porridge.

Z
Z
Z

Early to Bed

Early to bed,
Early to rise.
Makes little Johnny,
Wealthy and wise.

91

Twinkle, Twinkle, Little Star

Twinkle, twinkle, little star,
How I wonder what you are.
Up above the world so high,
Like a diamond in the sky.
Twinkle, twinkle, little star,
How I wonder what you are.

The Balloon

What is the news of the day,
Good neighbor, I pray?
They say the balloon,
Is gone up to the moon.
That is the news of the day.

92

A Star

Higher than a house,
Higher than a tree.
Oh, whatever can that be?
A star.

Starlight, Star Bright

Starlight, star bright,
The first star I see tonight.
I wish I may, I wish I might,
Have the wish I wish tonight.

There Were Ten in the Bed

There were ten in the bed and the little one said,
"Roll over. Roll over."
So they all rolled over and one fell out.

There were nine in the bed and the little one said,
"Roll over. Roll over."
So they all rolled over and one fell out.

There were eight in the bed and the little one said,
"Roll over. Roll over."
So they all rolled over and one fell out.

There were seven in the bed and the little one said,
"Roll over. Roll over."
So they all rolled over and one fell out.

There were six in the bed and the little one said,
"Roll over. Roll over."
So they all rolled over and one fell out.

There were five in the bed and the little one said,
"Roll over. Roll over."
So they all rolled over and one fell out.

There were four in the bed and the little one said,
"Roll over. Roll over."
So they all rolled over and one fell out.

There were three in the bed and the little one said,
"Roll over. Roll over."
So they all rolled over and one fell out.

There were two in the bed and the little one said,
"Roll over. Roll over."
So they all rolled over and one fell out.

There was one in the bed and the little one said,
"Goodnight."

Hippity-hop to Bed

Oh, it's hippity-hop to bed.
I'd rather sit up instead,
But when Father says, "Must",
There's nothing but just,
Go hippity-hop to bed.

Goodnight, Sleep Tight

Goodnight, sleep tight.
Wake up bright,
In the morning light,
To do what's right,
With all your might.